1, 2, I Love You

By Alice Schertle • Illustrated by Emily Arnold McCully

chronicle books · san francisco

Book design by Kristen M. Nobles.
Typeset in Bembo and Taub.
The illustrations in this book were rendered in watercolor
on Fabriano watercolor paper.
Manufactured in China

Library of Congress Cataloging-in-Publication Data
Schertle, Alice.
1, 2, I love you / by Alice Schertle; illustrated by Emily Arnold
McCully.
p. cm.
Summary: A counting rhyme that captures the playfulness
and tender affection between parent and child.
ISBN 0-8118-3518-9
[1. Counting. 2. Parent and child—Fiction. 3. Play—Fiction.
4. Stories in rhyme.] I. Title: One, two, I love you.
II. McCully, Emily Arnold, ill. III. Title.
PZ8.3.S29717Aae 2004
[E]—dc22
2003021245

Distributed in Canada by Raincoast Books
9050 Shaughnessy Street
Vancouver, British Columbia V6P 6E5

10 9 8 7 6 5 4 3 2 1

Chronicle Books LLC
85 Second Street
San Francisco, California 94105

www.chroniclekids.com

To 1, 2, 3 children: Jen, Kate and John;
and to 1, 2 grandchildren: Spence and Dylan

—A. S.

For Sasha's baby, Oliver, in San Francisco

—C. A. M.

1, 2, I love you.

I will give you stars
to jingle in your pockets
and to put in pickle jars.

3, 4, dip and pour

oceans from a pail.
We might catch a mermaid
with a swishy fish's tail.

5, 6, clickety sticks,

a trumpet and a drum,
I'll march with you to Timbuktu,
toot-toot tumpety-tum.

7, 8, celebrate—

I can make you fly.
Swing song, sing along,
you can touch the sky.

9, 10, little men

standing in a line.

"Let's be friends," says one of yours.

"Okay," says one of mine.

I love you from 1 to 10

and all the way back down again!

10, 9, 8, don't be late,

rattling down the track,
big old engine up in front,
little caboose in back.

7, 6, magic tricks,

watch us disappear.
We can hide all snug inside—
they'll *never* find us here.

5, 4, 3, you and me,

out in rainy weather.
Catch a rainbow in our hands,
we'll hold it up together.

2, 1, now we're done,

bucket's empty, good-bye sun,
trumpet's silent, drum is still,
shadows cover house and hill.

Little men all settled down.
Train has left for Noopy Town.
You and I begin to yawn.
Our boat is here, we're climbing on. . . .

Dip and sway, we catch the breeze
and sail away above the trees
to fall asleep among the stars
we sometimes keep in pickle jars.